THIS IGLOO BOOK BELONGS TO:

....

igloobooks

Published in 2017
by Igloo Books Ltd
Cottage Farm
Sywell
NN6 0BJ
www.igloobooks.com

Copyright © 2017 Igloo Books Ltd

LEO002 0717
2 4 6 8 10 9 7 5 3 1
ISBN 978-1-78670-962-2

Written by Melanie Joyce
Illustrated by David Creighton-Pester
Song lyrics by Melanie Joyce

Cover designed by Nicholas Gage
Interiors designed by Amy Bradford
Edited by Hannah Cather

Narrated by Michael Ball
Music, song vocals and sound by Sam Park

Printed and manufactured in China

WHO'S AFRAID OF THE DARK?

igloobooks

If you go into the dark
and tiptoe about at night,
nothing will look the same
as it does when it is light.

The sun will sink from the sky
and the moon will shine fat and round.

Shapes will creep from the wood and STRETCH along the ground.

But there's no need to worry,

or for you to be afraid.

The shapes are only shadows

that the branches or trees have made.

It's true, the dark is full of things that

CREAK and CRACK and MOAN.

Things that JUMP,
things that go BUMP
and things that
GRUMBLE and GROAN.

But you'll find it's just a badger, MUNCHING on a midnight snack,
SHUFFLING over twigs and sticks along the forest track.

Perhaps he'll stop for a chat
or play a game or two.
Then he'll be on his way,
wave goodbye and say,
"THANK YOU!"

If you do go into the dark,
always remember to look behind,
because lurking in the shadows,
who knows what you might find?
Bats could fly out of the trees
and get tangled in your hair,
or suddenly you'll hear a
SNAP and ask...

... "IS ANYBODY THERE?"

It will only be the night owl
SWOOPING through the sky.
HOO-HOO! he'll say to you,
as he goes flying by.

The fluffy owlets in the nest might sing a song for you.
They'll flap their little wings and go, TE-WIT, TE-WIT, TE-WOO!

But are there really monsters hiding in places you can't see?

And do you think to yourself,

"ARE THEY FOLLOWING ME?"

Don't worry, it's only the hedgehogs, SHUFFLING by the wall,
making their way back to their house, and not monsters after all.

If you go out into the dark
and miss the daytime sun...

... remember that playing in the
moonlight can really be lots of fun.

You can SPLASH in glittery pools
and watch the little fish.
If a shooting star ZOOMS by,
then you can make a magic wish.

When you hear a
SCRITCH and **SCRATCH**
or maybe a distant HOWL,
it will only be a guard dog
or maybe a kitty on the prowl.

You will hear noises at night
and wonder what they could be.
It doesn't mean they're scary,
just because you can't see.

So, if you're afraid of the dark
and think you should beware,
remember that you're not alone and
someone will always be there.

You'll get a hug and a kiss,

and maybe a story, too.

Then you'll yawn and know that

it really is bedtime for you.

You'll just curl up, safe and warm,
in the glow of the light,

and think of all the things
that you saw in the night.
You might hear a SNAP,
a HOOT, a CRACK or a BARK,
but you'll know just what it is
and won't be afraid of the dark.

Discover four more fantastic picture books on audio CD...

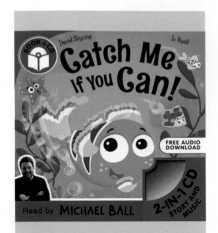

Catch Me If You Can!

It's race day and Terence the fish has got BIG fins to fill. Can he impress his dad and finally win the swimming race? Find out in this charming tale, all about being different.

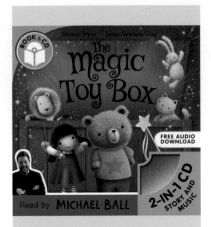

The Magic Toy Box

The clock has struck 12 and it's playtime for Lucy's adventurous toys. What will they get up to until morning? Enjoy this magical tale together at storytime.

Monkey Tricks

Join Marvin and Maddie as they have fun playing tricks on all their jungle friends. This hilarious book is perfect for a shared storytime, full of laughter.

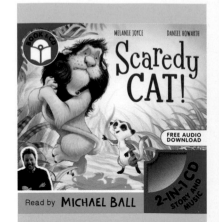

Scaredy Cat!

Lion is ready to leave the jungle, because he thinks he doesn't belong. Until, an unlikely little friend helps him believe in the power of friendship... and himself!

Scan the QR code below for your free audio download!

or visit https://igloobooks.com/picturebookandcd

igloobooks